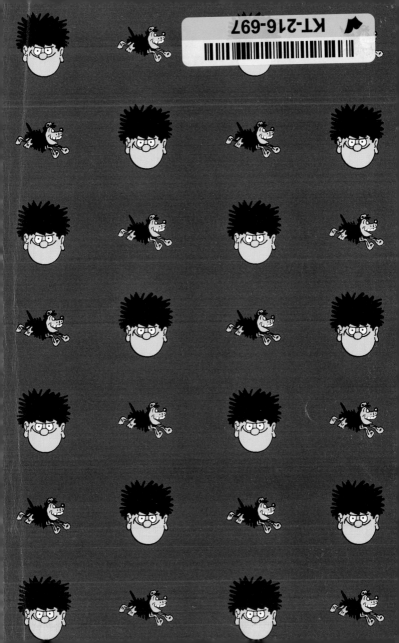

Ladybird books are widely available, but in case of
difficulty may be ordered by post or telephone from:

Ladybird Books – Cash Sales Department
Littlegate Road Paignton Devon TQ3 3BE
Telephone 0803 554761

A catalogue record for this book is available
from the British Library

Published by Ladybird Books Ltd Loughborough Leicestershire UK
Ladybird Books Inc Auburn Maine 04210 USA

Printed in EC

A SPLASHING TIME

Ladybird

"Phewww!" panted Dennis, his tongue hanging out.

"Whewww!" panted Gnasher, his tongue hanging out.

It was a scorching hot morning. Both Dennis and his faithful dog had woken with a raging thirst.

"C'mon Gnasher, Expedition Thirst Quencher!" gasped Dennis as he headed towards the kitchen. "I'm going to make myself a glass of menaceade!"

Gnasher bounded out into the front garden and started to dig furiously.

Gnasher knew that he had buried a large juicy bone somewhere in the front garden... but he wasn't sure where! The best thing to do was to start digging and see what would turn up.

Only a few flowerbeds and half the lawn had been turned over before Gnasher made his discovery. It looked like the juiciest bone of all time!

Gnasher's teeth snapped shut on the bone. The next second, a fierce jet of water crashed against the dog's legs and knocked him off the ground.

Dad was in the bathroom about to start his shave. A loud swooshing sound caused him to lean out of the window to see what was happening.

He was just in time to come face to face with Gnasher. The dog was lying on top of a forceful fountain of water that was shooting skyward at speed.

Dad made a desperate dive to grab the dog and pull him inside through the bathroom window.

YIKES!

Downstairs, Dennis had finally found various bottles of juice to mix a most unpleasant-looking concoction.

"Just add water," smiled Dennis, "and there's a glass of menaceade!"

He turned the tap, but nothing happened.

"Sheesh," said Dennis.

Next door, Walter was ready for a refreshing shower.

"I can try out my lovely flower fragrance bath soap," he twittered. He turned on the tap and nothing happened.

"Oh Mumsie!" wailed Walter.

"What's going on, Dad?" asked Dennis.

"Gnasher's bitten through the water main," said Dad, who was still holding the soaking wet dog. "I've phoned the repair men and all the water in our street has been turned off."

"But I was going to play with my water pistol," moaned Dennis... and then he had a great idea!

Within minutes Dennis came out of the house. He was wearing a cowboy hat and waving his favourite water pistol. Tied round his waist were the plastic bottles from the kitchen.

"What about a game?" grinned Dennis, barging into Walter's garden.

"Shall we play schools?" asked Walter innocently.

"Cowboys and Indians is much more fun," said Dennis. "I'll be the cowboys and you can be the Indians. Here's your outfit..."

Dennis pulled a feathered headdress firmly onto Walter's head and then squirted him with a water pistol full of raspberry juice.

"UGH!" cried Walter.

"Very good, Walter," laughed Dennis. "You're talking just like an Indian. Hope you enjoyed your shower!"

"Hee, hee!" chortled Dennis, as he and Gnasher made a hasty escape into the street. "The cordial makes great ammo for my water pistol! Now, who's next?"

Bully Bates was eating his way through a gigantic bag of toffees when he saw Dennis waving to him some distance down the street.

"Hmmm! He'll be after my sweets," thought Bully, "but he's got no chance!"

Suddenly, Gnasher's head appeared over the wall. Before Bully knew what was happening, his face was covered in lime juice!

"Oh, no!" cried Dennis. "You've eaten too many sweets, Bully. You must be feeling sick. Your face is green!"

"Ehh?" Bully looked at his face in a car wing mirror. "ARGHHH! It's true… Grooh! I do feel a bit unwell… Perhaps I shouldn't eat any more sweets."

"I'll take them then," chortled the Menace as he grabbed the bag. Before you could say 'sweet wrappers' Dennis and Gnasher were dashing away down the street.

AARGH!

GNEE!
GNEE!

Dennis eventually stopped running when he heard the magic word, 'drinks'. He went at once to investigate.

"Soggy Simpkins," he muttered, recognising the boy relaxing in a sunchair, "and with his new girlfriend. I think a touch of blackcurrant will do the trick."

As the girl went to the house for some drinks, Dennis aimed a series of short, sharp squirts at Soggy.

"Strange," said Simpkins, looking up to the sky. "Felt like rain on my face, yet there's not a cloud around." He didn't realise his face was covered in purple dots.

Soggy Simpkins thought that he was rather handsome. He couldn't understand what had happened when his girlfriend looked up at him, and then screamed in horror.

"It's horrible!" she cried, throwing the tray of drinks up in the air.

In the confusion that followed, Soggy tried to jump to his feet but only managed to collapse his sunchair. Dennis was on hand to catch the drinks, which he and Gnasher finished off in seconds.

"Nearly out of ammo," thought Dennis. "Just the lemon juice left. I'll head back and get a refill."

On reaching home he saw that the workmen were packing things away. "The water will be back on soon," one man said to Dennis.

"We may as well relax and wait for the water," Dennis said to Gnasher. Minutes later they were both fast asleep in the hot sunshine.

Meanwhile a small crowd of people had assembled at the front door.

"We've come to complain about Dennis and his water pistol," said Walter.

Suddenly, there was a loud yell from the back garden. Everyone raced to see what was happening.

The garden sprinkler had started up and soaked Dennis.

"Ho, ho!" roared the workman. "You must have left the sprinkler controls at 'on'…"

"And it started as soon as the water was connected," laughed Dad. "Still, it makes a smashing water pistol!"